International acclaim for ALLISON PEARSON's

I Don't Know How She Does It

"Sharp and witty, erudite and yet down-to-earth."
—*Los Angeles Times*

"The myth of 'having it all' has been mined by any number of writers, but none has ever produced as polished a gem as Allison Pearson's painfully funny first novel."
—*The Boston Globe*

"Wittily gives voice to the pull of progeny and partners, the longing for escape . . . and the fierce devotion to her children that tops every working mother's list. Makes us laugh and wince."
—*People*

"A book that made me howl with laughter."
—Maureen Freely, *The Times* (London)

"Refreshingly engaging. . . . Move[s] from farce to pathos in the course of a single paragraph."
—*Vogue*

"Kate Reddy is a smart, aggressive, wildly attractive heroine."
—*USA Today*

"A hilarious, pitch-perfect social commentary on the lives of working mothers. . . . Written with so much intelligence and humor that it's positively addicting."
—*The Plain Dealer*

ALLISON PEARSON

I Don't Know How She Does It

Allison Pearson, an award-winning journalist and author, is a staff writer for the London *Daily Telegraph*. Her first novel, *I Don't Know How She Does It*, became an international bestseller and was translated into thirty-two languages. It is now a major motion picture, adapted by Aline Brosh McKenna and starring Sarah Jessica Parker. Her most recent novel, *I Think I Love You*, is set to become a stage musical. Allison has given inspirational speeches around the world on women's issues and she can be contacted via her website www.allisonpearson.co.uk. She is a patron of Camfed, a charity that supports the education of thousands of African girls (www.camfed.org). Pearson lives in Cambridge with her husband and their two children.

Also by Allison Pearson

I Think I Love You

I Don't Know How She Does It

The Life of Kate Reddy, Working Mother

A Novel

ALLISON PEARSON

ANCHOR BOOKS

A DIVISION OF RANDOM HOUSE, INC.

NEW YORK

FIRST ANCHOR BOOKS EDITION, SEPTEMBER 2003

The Library of Congress has cataloged the Knopf edition as follows:
Pearson, Allison, 1960–
I don't know how she does it : the life of Kate Reddy, working mother / by
Allison Pearson.—1st ed.
p. cm.
1. Working mothers—Fiction. 2. Children of working mothers—Fiction.
3. Mother and child—Fiction. 4. London (England)—Fiction. I. Title.
PR6116.E17 I2 2002
823'.92—dc21
2002066104

Anchor ISBN: 0-375-71375-1

Book design by Robert C. Olsson

w w w . a n c h o r b o o k s . c o m

Printed in the United States of America
10 9 8 7 6 5 4 3 2 1

For Evie
with love

juggle: v. & n. **v. 1** *intr.* perform feats of dexterity, esp. by tossing objects in the air and catching them, keeping several in the air at the same time. **2** *tr.* continue to deal with (several activities) at once, esp. with ingenuity. **3** *intr. & tr.* (foll. by *with*) **a** deceive or cheat. **b** misrepresent (facts). **c** rearrange adroitly. **n. 1** a piece of juggling. **2** a fraud.

Concise Oxford Dictionary

PART ONE

1

Home

MONDAY, 1:37 A.M.   How did I get here? Can someone please tell me that? Not in this kitchen, I mean in this life. It is the morning of the school carol concert and I am hitting mince pies. No, let us be quite clear about this, I am *distressing* mince pies, an altogether more demanding and subtle process.

Discarding the Sainsbury luxury packaging, I winkle the pies out of their pleated foil cups, place them on a chopping board and bring down a rolling pin on their blameless floury faces. This is not as easy as it sounds, believe me. Hit the pies too hard and they drop a kind of fat-lady curtsy, skirts of pastry bulging out at the sides, and the fruit starts to ooze. But with a firm downward motion—imagine enough pressure to crush a small beetle—you can start a crumbly little landslide, giving the pastry a pleasing homemade appearance. And home-made is what I'm after here. Home is where the heart is. Home is where the good mother is, baking for her children.

All this trouble because of a letter Emily brought back from school ten days ago, now stuck on the fridge with a Tinky Winky magnet, asking if "parents could please make a voluntary contribution of appropriate festive refreshments" for the Christmas party they always put on after the carols. The note is printed in berry red and at the bottom, next to Miss Empson's signature, there is a snowman wearing a mortarboard and a shy grin. But do not be deceived by the strenuous tone of informality or the outbreak of chummy exclamation marks!!! Oh, no. Notes from school are written in code, a code buried so cunningly in the text that it could only be deciphered at Bletchley Park or by guilty women in the advanced stages of sleep deprivation.

Take that word "parents," for example. When they write "parents" what they really mean, what they still mean, is *mothers*. (Has a father who has a wife on the premises ever read a note from school? Technically, it's not impossible, I suppose, but the note will have been a party invitation and, furthermore, it will have been an invitation to a party that has taken place at least ten days earlier.) And "voluntary"? "Voluntary" is teacher-speak for "On pain of death and/or your child failing to gain a place at the senior school of your choice." As for "appropriate festive refreshments," these are definitely not something bought by a lazy cheat in a supermarket.

How do I know that? Because I still recall the look my own mother exchanged with Mrs. Frieda Davies in 1974, when a small boy in a dusty green parka approached the altar at Harvest Festival with two tins of Libby's cling peaches in a shoe box. The look was unforgettable. It said, What kind of sorry slattern has popped down to the Spar on the corner to celebrate God's bounty when what the good Lord clearly requires is a fruit medley in a basket with cellophane wrap? Or a plaited bread? Frieda Davies's bread, maneuvered the length of the church by her twins, was plaited as thickly as the tresses of a Rhinemaiden.

"You see, Katharine," Mrs. Davies explained later, doing that disapproving upsneeze thing with her sinuses over teacakes, "there are mothers who make an effort like your mum and me. And then you get the type of person who"—prolonged sniff—"don't make the effort."

Of course I knew who they were: Women Who Cut Corners. Even back in 1974, the dirty word had started to spread about mothers who went out to work. Females who wore trouser suits and even, it was alleged, allowed their children to watch television while it was still light. Rumors of neglect clung to these creatures like dust to their pelmets.

So before I was really old enough to understand what being a woman meant, I already understood that the world of women was divided in two: there were proper mothers, self-sacrificing bakers of apple pies and well-scrubbed invigilators of the washtub, and there were the other sort. At the age of thirty-five, I know precisely which kind I am, and I suppose that's what I'm doing here in the small hours of the thirteenth of December, hitting mince pies with a rolling pin till they look like something mother-made. Women used to have time to make mince pies and had to fake orgasms. Now we can manage the orgasms, but we have to fake the mince pies. And they call this progress.

"Damn. Damn. Where has Paula hidden the sieve?"

"Kate, what do you think you're doing? It's two o'clock in the morning!"

Richard is standing in the kitchen doorway, wincing at the light. Rich with his Jermyn Street pajamas, washed and tumbled to Babygro bobbliness. Rich with his acres of English reasonableness and his fraying kindness. Slow Richard, my American colleague Candy calls him, because work at his ethical architecture firm has slowed almost to a standstill, and it takes him half an hour to take the bin out and he's always telling me to slow down.

"Slow down, Katie, you're like that funfair ride. What's it called? The one where the screaming people stick to the side so long as the damn thing keeps spinning?"

"Centrifugal force."

"I know that. I meant what's the ride called?"

"No idea. Wall of Death?"

"Exactly."

I can see his point. I'm not so far gone that I can't grasp there has to be more to life than forging pastries at midnight. And tiredness. Deep-sea-diver tiredness, voyage-to-the-bottom-of-fatigue tiredness; I've never really come up from it since Emily was born, to be honest. Five years of walking round in a lead suit of sleeplessness. But what's the alternative? Go in to school this afternoon and brazen it out, slam a box of Sainsbury's finest down on the table of festive offerings? Then, to the Mummy Who's Never There and the Mummy Who Shouts, Emily can add the Mummy Who Didn't Make an Effort. Twenty years from now, when my daughter is arrested in the grounds of Buckingham Palace for attempting to kidnap the king, a criminal psychologist will appear on the news and say, "Friends trace the start of Emily Shattock's mental problems to a school carol concert where her mother, a shadowy presence in her life, humiliated her in front of her classmates."

"Kate? Hello?"

"I need the sieve, Richard."

"What for?"

"So I can cover the mince pies with icing sugar."

"Why?"

"Because they are too evenly colored, and everyone at school will know I haven't made them myself, that's why."

Richard blinks slowly, like Stan Laurel taking in another fine mess. "Not why icing sugar, why *cooking*? Katie, are you mad? You only got back from the States three hours ago. No one expects you to produce anything for the carol concert."

"Well, *I* expect me to." The anger in my voice takes me by surprise and I notice Richard flinch. "So, where has Paula hidden the sodding sieve?"

Rich looks older suddenly. The frown line, once an amused exclamation mark between my husband's eyebrows, has deepened and widened without my noticing into a five-bar gate. My lovely funny Richard, who once looked at me as Dennis Quaid looked at Ellen Barkin in *The Big Easy* and now, thirteen years into an equal, mutually supportive partnership, looks at me the way a smoking beagle looks at a medical researcher—aware that such experiments may need to be conducted for the sake of human progress but still somehow pleading for release.

"Don't shout." He sighs. "You'll wake them." One candy-striped arm gestures upstairs where our children are asleep. "Anyway, Paula hasn't hidden it. You've got to stop blaming the nanny for everything, Kate. The sieve lives in the drawer next to the microwave."

"No, it lives right here in this cupboard."

"Not since 1997 it doesn't."

"Are you implying that I haven't used my own sieve for three years?"

"Darling, to my certain knowledge you have never met your sieve. Please come to bed. You have to be up in five hours."

Seeing Richard go upstairs, I long to follow him but I can't leave the kitchen in this state. I just can't. The room bears signs of heavy fighting; there is Lego shrapnel over a wide area, and a couple of mutilated Barbies—one legless, one headless—are having some kind of picnic on our tartan travel rug, which is still matted with grass from its last outing on Primrose Hill in August. Over by the vegetable rack, on the floor, there is a heap of raisins which I'm sure was there the morning I left for the airport. Some things have altered in my absence: half a dozen apples have been added to the big glass bowl on the pine table that sits next to the doors leading out to the garden, but no one has thought to discard the old fruit beneath and the pears at the bottom have started weeping a sticky amber resin. As I throw each pear in the bin, I shudder a little at the touch of rotten flesh. After washing and drying the bowl, I carefully wipe any stray amber goo off the apples and put them back. The whole operation takes maybe seven minutes. Next I start to swab the drifts of icing sugar off the stainless steel worktop, but the act of scouring releases an evil odor. I sniff the dishcloth. Slimy with bacteria, it has the sweet sickening stench of dead-flower water. Exactly how rancid would a dishcloth have to be before someone else in this house thought to throw it away?

I ram the dishcloth in the overflowing bin and look under the sink for a new one. There is no new one. Of course, there is no new one, Kate, you haven't been here to buy a new one. Retrieve old dishcloth from the bin and soak it in hot water with a dot of bleach. All I need to do now is put Emily's wings and halo out for the morning.

Have just turned off the lights and am starting up the stairs when I have a bad thought. If Paula sees the Sainsbury's cartons in the bin, she will spread news of my Great Mince Pie forgery on the nanny grapevine. Oh, hell. Retrieving the cartons from the bin, I wrap them inside yesterday's paper and carry the bundle at arm's length out through the front door. Looking right and left to make sure I am unobserved, I slip them into the big black sack in front of the house. Finally, with the evidence of my guilt disposed of, I follow my husband up to bed.

Through the landing window and the December fog, a crescent moon is reclining in its deck chair over London. Even the moon gets to put its feet up once a month. Man in the Moon, of course. If it was a Woman in the Moon, she'd never sit down. Well, would she?

I take my time brushing my teeth. A count of twenty for each molar. If I stay in the bathroom long enough, Richard will fall asleep and will not try to have sex with me. If we don't have sex, I can skip a shower in the morning. If I skip the shower, I will have time to start on the e-mails that have built up while I've been away and maybe even get some presents bought on the way to work. Only ten shopping days to Christmas, and I am in possession of precisely nine gifts, which leaves twelve to get plus stocking fillers for the children. And still no delivery from KwikToy, the rapid on-line present service.

"Kate, are you coming to bed?" Rich calls from the bedroom.

His voice sounds slurry with sleep. Good.

"I have something I need to talk to you about. Kate?"

"In a minute," I say. "Just going up to make sure they're OK."

I climb the flight of stairs to the next landing. The carpet is so badly frayed up here that the lip of each step looks like the dead grass you find under a marquee five days after a wedding. Someone's going to have an accident one of these days. At the top, I catch my breath and silently curse these tall thin London houses. Standing in the stillness outside the children's doors, I can hear their different styles of sleeping—his piglet snufflings, her princess sighs.

When I can't sleep and, believe me, I would dream of sleep if my mind weren't too full of other stuff for dreams, I like to creep into Ben's room and sit on the blue chair and just watch him. My baby looks as though he has hurled himself at unconsciousness, like a very small man trying to leap aboard an accelerating bus. Tonight, he's sprawled the length of the cot on his front, arms extended, tiny fingers curled round an invisible pole. Nestled to his cheek is the disgusting kangaroo that he worships—a shelf full of the finest stuffed animals an anxious parent can buy, and what does he choose to love? A cross-eyed marsupial from Woolworth's remainder bin. Ben can't tell us when he's tired yet, so he simply says Roo instead. He can't sleep without Roo because Roo to him *means* sleep.

It's the first time I've seen my son in four days. Four days, three nights. First there was the trip to Stockholm to spend some face time with a jumpy new client, then Rod Task called from the office and told me to get my ass over to New York and hold the hand of an old client who needed reassuring that the new client wasn't taking up too much of my time.

Benjamin never holds my absences against me. Too little still. He always greets me with helpless delight like a fan windmilling arms at a Hollywood premiere. Not his sister, though. Emily is five years old and full of jealous wisdom. Mummy's return is always the cue for an intricate sequence of snubs and punishments.

"Actually, Paula reads me that story."

"But I want Dadda to give me a bath."

Wallis Simpson got a warmer welcome from the Queen Mother than I get from Emily after a business trip. But I bear it. My heart sort of pleats inside and somehow I bear it. Maybe I think I deserve it.

I leave Ben snoring softly and gently push the door of the other room. Bathed in the candied glow of her Cinderella light, my daughter is, as is her preference, naked as a newborn. (Clothes, unless you count bridal or princess wear, are a constant irritation to her.) When I pull the duvet up, her legs twitch in protest like a laboratory frog. Even when she was a baby, Emily couldn't stand being covered. I bought her one of those zip-up sleep bags, but she thrashed around in it and blew out her cheeks like the God of Wind in the corner of old maps, till I had to admit defeat and gave it away. Even in sleep, when my girl's face has the fuzzy bloom of an apricot, you can see the determined jut to her chin. Her last school report said, *Emily is a very competitive little girl and will need to learn to lose more gracefully.*

"Remind you of anyone, Kate?" said Richard and let out that trodden-puppy yelp he has developed lately.

There have been times over the past year when I have tried to explain to my daughter—I felt she was old enough to hear this—why Mummy has to go to work. Because Mum and Dad both need to earn money to pay for our house and for all the things she enjoys doing like ballet lessons and going on holiday. Because Mummy has a job she is good at and it's really important for women to work as well as men. Each time the speech builds to a stirring climax—trumpets, choirs, the tearful sisterhood waving flags—in which I assure Emily that she will understand all this when she is a big girl and wants to do interesting things herself.

Unfortunately, the case for equal opportunities, long established in liberal Western society, cuts no ice in the fundamentalist regime of the five-year-old. There is no God but Mummy, and Daddy is her prophet.

In the morning, when I'm getting ready to leave the house, Emily asks the same question over and over until I want to hit her and then, all the way to work, I want to cry for having wanted to hit her.

"Are you putting me to bed tonight? Is Mummy putting me to bed tonight? Are you? Who is putting me to bed tonight? Are you, Mum, are you?"

Do you know how many ways there are of saying the word *no* without actually using the word *no*? I do.

MUST REMEMBER

Angel wings. Quote for new stair carpet. Take lasagne out of freezer for Saturday lunch. Buy kitchen roll, stainless-steel special polish thingy, present and card for Harry's party. How old is Harry? Five? Six? Must get organized with well-stocked present drawer like proper mother. Buy Christmas tree and stylish lights recommended in *Telegraph* (Selfridge's or Habitat? Can't remember. Damn). Nanny's Christmas bribe/present (Eurostar ticket? Cash? DKNY?). Emily wants Baby Wee-Wee doll (over my dead body). Present for Richard (Wine-tasting? Arsenal? Pajamas?), In-laws' book—The Lost Gardens of Somewhere? Ask Richard to collect dry cleaning. Office party, what to wear? Black velvet too small. Stop eating *now*. Fishnets lilac. Leg wax no time, shave instead. Book stress-busting massage. Highlights must book soonest (starting to look like mid-period George Michael). Pelvic floor *squeeeeze*! Supplies of Pill!!! Ice cake (royal icing?—chk Delia). Cranberries. Mini party sausages. Stamps for cards. Second class × 40. Present for E's teacher? And, whatever you do, wean Ben off dummy before Xmas with in-laws. Chase KwikToy, useless mail-order present company. Smear test NB. Wine, Gin. Vin santo. Ring Mum. Where did I put Simon Hopkinson "dry with hair dryer" goose recipe? Stuffing? Hamster???

2

Work

6:37 A.M. "Oh, come let us a-door him. Oh, come let us a-door him. Oh, come let us a-door hi-mmm!" I am stroked, tugged and, when that doesn't work, finally Christmas-caroled awake by Emily. She is standing by my side of the bed and she wants to know where her present is. "You can't buy their love," says my mother-in-law, who obviously never threw enough cash at the problem.

I did once try to come home empty-handed from a business trip, but on the way back from Heathrow I lost my nerve and got the cab to stop at Hounslow where I dived into a Toys "Я" Us, adding a toxic shimmer to my jet lag. Emily's global Barbie collection is now so sensationally slutty, it can only be a matter of time before it becomes a Jeff Koons exhibit. Flamenco Barbie, AC Milan Barbie (soccer strip, dinky boots), Thai Barbie—a flexible little minx who can bend over backwards and suck her own toes—and the one that Richard calls Klaus Barbie, a terrifying *über*-blonde with sightless blue eyes in jodhpurs and black boots.

"Mummy," says Emily, weighing up her latest gift with a connoisseur's eye, "this fairy Barbie could wave a wand and make the little Baby Jesus not be cross."

"Barbie isn't in the Baby Jesus story, Emily."

She shoots me her best Hillary Clinton look, full of noble this-pains-me-more-than-you condescension. "Not *that* Baby Jesus." She sighs. "Another one, silly."

You see, what you can buy from a five-year-old when you get back from a client visit is, if not love or even forgiveness, then an amnesty of sorts. Entire minutes when the need to blame is briefly overcome by the need to rip open a package in a tantrum of glee. (Any working mother who says she doesn't bribe her kids can add Liar to her CV.) Emily now has a gift to mark each occasion of her mother's infidelity—playing away with her career—just as my mum got a new charm for her bracelet every time my father played away with other women. By the time Dad walked out when I was thirteen, Mum could barely lift the golden handcuff on her wrist.

Am lying here thinking things could be a lot worse—at least my husband is not an alcoholic serial adulterer—when Ben toddles into the bedroom and I can hardly believe what I'm seeing.

"Oh, God, Richard, what's happened to his hair?"

Rich peers over the top of the duvet, as though noticing his son, who will be one in January, for the first time. "Ah. Paula took him to that place by the garage. Said it was getting in his eyes."

"He looks like something out of the Hitler Youth."

"Well, it will grow back, obviously. And Paula thought, and I thought too, obviously, that the whole Fauntleroy ringlet thing— well, it's not how kids look these days, is it?"

"He's not a *kid*. He's my baby. And it's how I want him to look. Like a baby."

Lately, I notice Rich has adopted a standard procedure for dealing with my rages. A sort of bowed-head-in-the-event-of-nuclear-attack submissive posture, but this morning he can't suppress a mutinous murmur.

"Don't think we could arrange an international conference call with the hairdresser at short notice."

"And what's that supposed to mean?"

"It just means you've got to learn to let go, Kate." And with one practiced movement, he scoops up the baby, swipes the gangrenous snot from his tiny nose and heads downstairs for breakfast.

7:15 A.M. The change of gears between work and home is so abrupt sometimes that I swear I can hear the crunch of mesh in my brain. It takes a while to get back onto the children's wavelength. Brimming with good intentions, I start off in Julie Andrews mode, all tennis-club enthusiasm and mad singsong emphases.

"*Now*, children, what would you *like* for *break*-fast to-*day*?"

Emily and Ben humor this kindly stranger for a while until Ben can take no more of it and stands up in his high chair, reaches out, and pinches my arm as though to make sure it's me. Their relief is plain as, over the next frazzled half hour, the ratty bag they know as Mummy comes back. "You're having Shreddies and that's it! No, we haven't got Fruitibix. I don't care what Daddy let you have."

Richard has to leave early: a site visit with a client in Battersea. Can I do the handover with Paula? Yes, but only if I can leave at 7:45 on the dot.

7:57 A.M.   And here she comes, flourishing the multiple excuses of the truly unapologetic. The traffic, the rain, the alignment of the stars. You know how it is, Kate. Indeed I do. I cluck and sigh in the designated sympathy pauses while my nanny makes herself a cup of coffee and flicks without interest through my paper. Pointing out that in the twenty-six months Paula has been our children's carer she has managed to be late every fourth morning would be to risk a row, and a row would contaminate the air that my children breathe. So no, there won't be a row. Not today. Three minutes to get to the bus, eight minutes' walk away.

8:27 A.M.   I am going to be late for work. Indecently, intrepidly late. Bus lane is full of buses. Abandon bus. Make lung-scorching sprint down City Road and then cut across Finsbury Square, where my heels skewer into the forbidden grass and I attract the customary loud *Oy!* from the old guy whose job it is to shout at you for running across the grass.

"Oy, miss! Cancha go round the outside like everyone else?"

Being shouted at is embarrassing, but I am beginning to worry that a small shameful part of me really likes being called *miss* in a public place. At the age of thirty-five and with gravity and two small children dragging you down, you have to take your compliments where you can. Besides, I reckon the shortcut saves me maybe two and a half minutes.

8:47 A.M.   One of the City's oldest and most distinguished institutions, Edwin Morgan Forster stands at the corner of Broadgate and St. Anthony's Lane; a nineteenth-century fortress with a great jutting prow of twentieth-century glass, it looks as though a liner has crashed into a department store and come out the other side. Approaching the main entrance, I slow to a trot and run through my kit inspection:

Shoes, matching, two of? Check.
No baby sick on jacket? Check.
Skirt not tucked into knickers? Check.
Bra not visible? Check.

OK, I'm going in. Stride briskly across the marble atrium and flash my pass at Gerald in Security. Since the revamp eighteen months ago, the lobby of Edwin Morgan Forster, which used to look like a bank, now resembles one of those zoo enclosures designed by Russian constructivists to house penguins. Every surface is an eyeball-shattering arctic white except the back wall, which is painted the exact turquoise of the Yardley gift soap favored by my Great-aunt Phyllis thirty years ago, but which was described by the designer as an "oceangoing color of vision and futurity." For this piece of wisdom, a firm which is paid to manage other people's money handed over an unconfirmed seven hundred and fifty thousand dollars.

Can you believe this building? Seventeen floors served by four lifts. Divide by four hundred and thirty employees, factor in six button-pushing ditherers, two mean bastards who won't hold the door, and Rosa Klebb with a sandwich trolley, and you either have a possible four-minute wait or take the stairs. I take the stairs.

Arrive on Floor 13 with fuchsia face and walk straight into Robin Cooper-Clark, our pinstriped Director of Investment. The clash of odors is as immediate as it is pungent—me: Eau de Sweat, him: Floris Elite with under-notes of Winchester and walnut dashboard.

Robin is exceptionally tall, and it is one of his gifts that he manages to look down at you without actually looking down *on* you—without making you feel in any way small. It came as no surprise to learn in an obituary last year that his father was a bishop with a Military Cross. Robin has something both saintly and indestructible about him; there have been times at EMF when I have thought I would die if it weren't for his kindness and lightly mocking respect.

"Remarkable color, Kate, been skiing?" Robin's mouth is twitching up at the corners and on its way to a smile, but one bushy gray eyebrow arches incredulously towards the clock above the dealing desk.

Can I risk pretending that I've been in since seven and just slipped out for a cappuccino? A glance across the office tells me that my assistant, Guy, is already smirking purposefully by the watercooler. Damn. Guy must have spotted me at exactly the same moment because, across the bowed heads of the traders, phones cradled under their chins, over the secretaries and the European desk and the Global Equities team in their identical purple Lewin's shirts, comes the Calling-All-Superiors voice of my assistant. "I've put the document from Bengt Bergman on your desk, Katharine," he announces. "Sorry to see you've had problems getting in again."

Notice that use of the word "again," the drop of poison on the tip of the dagger. Little creep. When we funded Guy Chase through the European Business School three years ago, he was a Balliol brain ache with a four-piece suit and a personal hygiene deficit. He came back wearing charcoal Armani and the expression of someone with a Master's in Blind Ambition. I think I can honestly say that Guy is the only man at Edwin Morgan Forster who likes the fact that I have kids. Chicken pox, summer holidays, carol concerts—all are opportunities for Guy to shine in my absence. I can see Robin Cooper-Clark looking at me expectantly now. Think, Kate, think.

It is possible to get away with being late in the City. The key thing is to offer what my lawyer friend Debra calls a Man's Excuse. Senior managers who would be frankly appalled by the story of a vomiting nocturnal baby or an AWOL nanny (mysteriously, child care, though paid for by both parents, is always deemed to be the female's responsibility) are happy to accept anything to do with the internal combustion engine.

"The car broke down/was broken into."

"You should have seen the"—*fill in scene of mayhem*—"at"—*fill in street*.

Either of these will do very well. Car alarms have been a valuable recent addition to the repertoire of male excuses because, although displaying female symptoms—hair-trigger unpredictability, high-pitched shrieking—they are attached to a Man's Excuse and can be taken to a garage to be fixed.

"You should have seen the mess at Dalston Junction," I tell Robin, composing my features into a mask of stoic urban resignation and, with outstretched arms, indicating a whole vista of car carnage. "Some maniac in a white van. Traffic lights out of sync. Unbelievable. Must have been stuck there—oh, twenty minutes."

He nods. "London driving almost makes one grateful for Network Southeast."

There is a heartbeat of a pause . . . a pause in which I try to ask about the health of Jill Cooper-Clark, who was diagnosed with breast cancer in the summer. But Robin is one of those Englishmen equipped from birth with an early-warning system which helps them to intercept and deflect any incoming questions of a personal nature. So even as my lips are forming his wife's name, he says, "I'll get Christine to book a lunch for us, Kate. You know they've converted some cellar by the Old Bailey—serving up lightly grilled witness, no doubt. Sounds amusing, don't you think?"

"Yes, I was just wondering how—"

"Splendid. Talk later."

By the time I reach the haven of my desk, I've regained my composure. Here's the thing: I love my job. It may not always sound like it, but I do. I love the blood-rush when the stocks I took a punt on deliver the goods. I get a kick out of being one of the handful of women in the Club Lounge at the airport, and, when I get back, I love sharing my travel horror stories with friends. I love the hotels with room service that appears like a genie and the prairies of white cotton that give me the sleep I crave. (When I was younger I wanted to go to bed with other people; now that I have two children my fiercest desire is to go to bed with myself for a whole twelve hours.) Most of all I love the work: the synapse-snapping satisfaction of being good at it, of being in control when the rest of life seems such an awful mess. I love the fact that the numbers do what I say and never ask why.

9:03 A.M. Switch on my computer and wait for it to connect. The network is so slow this morning it would be quicker to fly to Hong

Kong and pick up the Hang bloody Seng in person. Type in my password—Ben Pampers—and go straight into Bloomberg to see what the markets have been up to overnight. The Nikkei is steady, Brazil's Bovespa is doing its usual crazy samba, while the Dow Jones looks like the printout on a do-not-resuscitate patient in intensive care. Baby, it's cold outside, and not just on account of the fog nuzzling the office blocks outside my window.

Next, I check currencies for any dramatic movements, then type in TOP to call up all the big corporate news stories. The main one is about Gayle Fender, a bond trader or, rather, an ex-trader. She's suing her firm, Lawrence Austen, for sex discrimination because male colleagues got far bigger bonuses than she did for less good results. The headline reads: ICE MAIDEN COOLS TOWARDS MEN. As far as the media is concerned, City women are all either Elizabeth I or a resting lap dancer. That old virgin-and-whore thing wrapped up in the *Wall Street Journal*.

Personally, I've always fancied the idea of becoming an Ice Maiden—maybe you can buy the outfit? Trimmed in white fur, stalactite heels with matching pickax. Anyway, Gayle Fender's story will end how those stories always end: with a *No comment* as, eyes lowered, she leaves a courtroom by a side door. This City smothers dissent: we have ways of making you not talk. Stuffing people's mouths with fifty-pound notes tends to do the trick.

Click on e-mails. Forty-nine arrivals in my Inbox since I left on Thursday. Skim down them, sorting out the junk first.

Free trial of a new investment magazine? Trash.

You are invited to a conference on globalization on the shores of Lake Geneva catered by the world-famous chef Jean-Louis. . . . Trash.

Human Resources wants to know if I will appear in the new EMF corporate video. Only if I get my own trailer with John Cusack tied to the bed.

Will I sign a card for some poor bugger in Treasury who's been made redundant? (Jeff Brooks is going voluntarily, they say, but the compulsories will start soon.) Yes.

The message at the very top of the Inbox is from Celia Harmsworth, head of Human Resources. It says that my boss Rod Task has had to pull out of the induction talk for EMF's trainees this lunchtime and could I please step in? "We would be very glad to see you in the thirteenth-floor conference room from 1 p.m.!"

No, no, no! I have nine fund reports to write by Friday. Plus I have a very important nativity play to attend at 2:30 this afternoon.

With work memos out of the way, I can get to the real e-mails, the ones that matter: messages from friends, jokes and stories handed around the world like sweets. If it's really true what they say, that mine is the time-famished generation, then e-mail is our guilty snack, our comfort food. It would be hard to explain how much sustenance I get from my regular correspondents. There's Debra, my best friend from college, now mother of two and a lawyer with Addison Pope, just across the way from the Bank of England and about ten minutes' walk from Edwin Morgan Forster. Not that I ever get down there to see her. Might as well work on Pluto. And then there's Candy, foul-mouthed fellow fund manager, World Wide Web whiz and proud export of Rockaway, New Jersey, Candace Marlene Stratton. My sister-in-arms and a woman in the vanguard of the latest developments in world corsetry. My favorite character in literature is Rosalind in *As You Like It;* Candy's favorite character in literature is the guy in Elmore Leonard who wears a T-shirt that says YOU'VE OBVIOUSLY MISTAKEN ME FOR SOMEONE WHO GIVES A SHIT.

Candy sits right over there, next to the pillar, fifteen feet away, and yet we scarcely exchange more than a few words out loud during an average day. On-screen, though, we're in and out of each other's minds like old-fashioned neighbors.

To: Kate Reddy, EMF
From: Candy Stratton

K8,

Q: Why are married women heavier than single women?

A: Single women come home, see what's in the fridge, and go to bed. Married women come home, see what's in bed, and go to the fridge.

How U? Me: Cystitis. Too much SX xxxx

I decided not to approach Rod Task in person over the question of leaving work early to get to Emily's nativity play. Better to tag it on casually as a PS to some work e-mail. Make it look like a fact of life, not a favor. Just got a reply.

To: Kate Reddy
From: Rod Task

Jesus, Katie, only seems like yesterday you had your own nativity.

Sure, take the time you need, but we should talk c. 5:30. And I need you to go to Stockholm to hold Sven's hand again. Is Friday good for you, Beaut?

Cheers, Rod

No, Friday is not good for me. I can't believe he expects me to do another trip before Christmas. Means I will miss the office party, have to cancel lunch with Debra again, and lose the shopping time I was counting on.

Our office is open-plan but the Director of Marketing has one of two rooms with walls; the other belongs to Robin Cooper-Clark. When I march in to Rod to make my protest, the office is empty, but I stay a few moments anyway to take in the view through the floor-to-ceiling window. Directly below is the Broadgate rink, a dinner plate of ice set in the middle of staggered towers of concrete and steel. At this hour, it's empty save for a lone skater, a tall dark guy in a green sweatshirt, carving out what at first I think are figures of eight but, as he makes the long downward stroke, realize is a large dollar sign. With the fog unfurling, the City looks as it did during the Blitz, when smoke from the fires dispersed, magically revealing the dome of St. Paul's. Turn in the opposite direction and you see the Canary Wharf tower winking like a randy Cyclops.

Coming out of Rod's room, I run smack into Celia Harmsworth, although no injury is done to either party because I simply bounce off Celia's stupendous bust. When Englishwomen of a certain background reach the age of fifty, they no longer have breasts, they have a bosom or even, depending on acreage of land and antiquity of lineage, a bust. Breasts come in twos, but a bust is always singular; the pliant pair meld into a fiberglass monopod sloping gently downward like a continental shelf. The bust denies the possibility of cleavage or any kind of jiggling. Where breasts say, *Come and play,* the bust, like the snub nose of a bumper car, says, *Out of my way!* The Queen has a bust and so does Celia Harmsworth.

"Katharine Reddy, always in such a hurry," she scolds. As head of Human Resources, Celia is effortlessly one of the least human people in the building; childless, charmless, chilly as Chablis, she has this knack of making you feel both useless and used. When I went back to work after Emily was born, I found out that Chris Bunce, hedge-fund manager and EMF's biggest earner for the past two years, had put a shot of vodka in the expressed breast milk I was storing in the office fridge next to the lifts. I approached Celia and asked her, woman to woman, what course of action she suggested taking against a jerk who, when confronted by me in Davy's Bar, claimed that putting alcohol into the food intended for a nine-week-old baby was " 'Avin' a bit of a larf."

I can still remember the moue of distaste on Celia's face, and it wasn't for that bastard Bunce. "Use your feminine wiles, dear," she said.

Celia tells me she is delighted that I can talk to the trainees at lunchtime. "Rod said you could do the presentation in your sleep. Just slides and a few sandwiches, you know the drill, Kate. And don't forget the Mission Statement, will you?"

I make a quick calculation. If the induction lasts an hour including drinks, say, that will leave me thirty minutes to find a cab and get across the City to Emily's school for the start of the nativity play. Should be enough time. I can make it so long as they don't ask any damn questions.

1:01 P.M. "Good afternoon, ladies and gentlemen, my name is Kate Reddy and I'd like to welcome you all to the thirteenth floor. Thirteen is unlucky for some, but not here at Edwin Morgan Forster, which ranks in the top ten money managers in the UK and in the top fifty globally in terms of assets, and which, for five years running, has been voted money manager of the year. Last year, we generated revenue in excess of £300 million, which explains why absolutely no expense has been spared on the fabulous tuna sandwiches you see spread out before you today."

Rod's right. I can do this sort of stuff in my sleep; in fact, I pretty much *am* doing it in my sleep as the jet lag takes hold and the crown of my skull starts to tighten and my legs feel as though someone is filling them with iced water.

"You will, I'm sure, already be familiar with the term 'fund manager.' Put at its simplest, a fund manager is a high-class gambler. My job is to study the form of companies round the world, assess the going rate in the markets for their products, check out the track record of jockeys, stick a big chunk of money on the best bet, and then hope to hell that they don't fall at the first fence."

There is laughter around the room, the overgrateful laughter of twentysomethings caught between arrogance at securing one of only six EMF traineeships and wetting themselves at the thought of being found out.

"If the horses I've backed do fall, I have to decide whether we shoot them right away or whether it's worth nursing that broken leg back to health. Remember, ladies and gentlemen, compassion can be expensive, but it's not necessarily a waste of your money."

I was a trainee myself twelve years ago, sitting in a room just like this one, crossing and uncrossing my legs, unsure whether it was worse to look like the Duchess of Kent or Sharon Stone. The only woman recruit in my year, I was surrounded by guys, big animal guys at ease in their pinstriped pelts. Not like me: the black crepe Whistles suit I had spent my last forty quid on made me look like a Wolverhampton schools inspector.

This year's bunch of novices is pretty typical: four guys, two girls. The guys always slouch at the back; the girls sit upright in the front row, pens poised to take notes they will never need. You get to know the types after a while. Look at Mr. Anarchist over there with the Velcro sideburns and the Liam Gallagher scowl. In a suit today, but mentally still wearing a leather jacket, Dave was probably some kind of student activist at college. He read economics the better to arm himself for the workers' struggle while morally blackmailing all the kids on his corridor into buying that undrinkable Rwandan coffee. Right now, he's sitting there telling himself he's just going to do this City shit for two years, five tops. Get some serious dough behind him, then launch his humanitarian crusade. I almost feel sorry for him. Seven years down the line, living in some modernist mausoleum in Notting Hill, school fees for two kids, wife with a ruinous Jimmy Choo habit, Dave will be nodding off in front of *Friends* like the rest of us, with a copy of the *New Statesman* unopened in his lap.

The other guys are pink-gilled landed types with prep-school partings. The one called Julian has an Adam's apple so overactive it's practically making cider. As usual, the girls are unmistakably women, whereas the men are barely more than boys. Between them, EMF's two female trainees cover the spectrum of womanhood. One is a doughy Shires girl with a kindly bun face and a velvet headband, the daytime tiara of her class. Clarissa somebody. Glance down the list of potted biographies and see that Clarissa is a graduate in Modern Studies from the University of Peterborough. Pure back-office material. Must be a niece of one of the directors; you don't get into EMF with a degree like that unless you're a blood relative of money.

The girl next to her looks more interesting. Born and brought up in Sri Lanka but educated at Cheltenham Ladies and the London School of Economics, one of those granddaughters of Empire who end up more English than the English—the sweetness of their courtesy, the decorum of their grammar. With catlike composure and remarkable leaf-shaped eyes that gaze steadily out through tortoiseshell specs, Momo Gumeratne is so pretty she should only enter the Square Mile with an armed guard.

The trainees return my appraising stare. I wonder what they see. Blondish hair, decent legs, in good enough shape not to be pinned for a mother. They wouldn't guess I was northern, either (accent ironed out when I came to study down south). They may even be a little scared of me. The other day Rich said I frightened him sometimes.

"Now, I'm sure everyone here will have seen that line they put in tiny bottom-row-of-the-optician's-chart print on your bank and building society accounts? 'Remember that the value of your investment can go down as well as up.' Yes? Well, that's me. If I pick 'em wrong, the value goes down, so at EMF we do our very best to ensure that doesn't happen and most of the time we succeed. I find it useful to bear in mind when I'm selling three million dollars of airline stock, as I did this morning, that ours is the only flutter in the world which can leave a little old lady in Dumbarton without a pension. But don't worry, Julian, trainees are limited in the size of the deal they can make. We'll give you fifty grand for starters, just to get some practice."

Julian's cheeks flush from smoked trout to strawberry and the doughy girl's hand shoots up. "Can you tell me why you sold that particular stock today?"

"That's a very good question, Clarissa. Well, I had a four-million-dollar holding and the price was up and was continuing to rise, but we'd made a lot of money already and I knew from reading the trade papers that there was bad news coming about airlines. The job of fund manager is to get our clients' money out *before* the price weakens. All the time, I'm trying to balance the good things that might happen against the Act of an Almighty Pissed-Off God that may be lurking just around the corner."

In my experience, the biggest test for any Edwin Morgan Forster trainee is not the ability to grasp the essentials of investment or to secure a pass for the car park. No, the thing that shows what you're really made of is if you can keep a straight face the first time you hear the firm's Mission Statement. Known internally as the five pillars of wisdom, the Mission Statement is the primest corporate baloney. (By what freak of logic did hard-core capitalists of the late twentieth century end up parroting slogans first chanted by Maoist peasants who were not even permitted to own their own bicycles?)

"Our Five Pillars of Wisdom are (1) pulling together, (2) mutual honesty, (3) best results, (4) client care and (5) commitment to success!"

I can see Dave struggling manfully to suppress a smirk. Good boy. Glance up at the clock. Shit. Time to go. "Now, if there are no more questions—"

Damn. The other girl has her hand up now. At least you can rely on the men not to ask a question—even when they don't know anything, like this lot, and especially not of someone at my level, when asking a question means admitting that there are still things in the world that are beyond you.

"I'm so sorry," the young Sri Lankan begins, as though apologizing for some error she has yet to commit. "I know that EMF has—well, as a woman, Ms. Reddy, can you tell me honestly, how do you find working in this job?"

"Well, Ms.—?"

"Momo Gumeratne."

"Well, Momo, there are sixty fund managers here and only three of us are women. EMF does have an equal opportunities policy and as long as trainees like you keep coming through we're going to make that happen in practice.

"Secondly, I understand that the Japanese are working on a tank where you can grow babies outside the womb. They should have that perfected by the time you're ready to have children, Ms. Gumeratne, so we really will be able to have the first lunch-hour baby. Believe me, that would make everyone at Edwin Morgan Forster very happy."

I assume that will stop the questions dead, but Momo is not as mousy as I thought. Her coffee skin suffused with a blush, she puts up her hand again. As I turn to pick up my bag, indicating that the session is over, she starts to speak.

"I'm really sorry, Ms. Reddy, but may I ask if you have children of your own?"

No, she can't. "Yes, the last time I looked there were two of them. And may I suggest, Ms. Gumeratne, that you don't start your sentences with *I'm sorry*. There are a lot of words you'll find useful in this building, but sorry isn't one of them. Now, if that's all I really must go and check the markets—winners to pick, money to manage! Thank you for your attention, ladies and gentlemen, and please do come up if you see me round the building, and I'll test you on our Five Pillars of Wisdom. If you're really lucky, I'll give you my personal Pillar Number Six."

They look at me dumbly.

"Pillar Number Six: If money responds to your touch, then there's no limit to what a woman can achieve in this City. Money doesn't know what sex you are."

2:17 P.M. You can always pick up a cab from the rank outside Warburg's. Any day except today. Today the cabbies are all at some dedicated Make Kate Late rally. After seven minutes of not being hysterical at the curbside, I hurl myself in front of a taxi with its light off. The driver swerves to avoid me. I tell him I'll double the fare on the clock if he takes me to Emily's school without using his brakes. Lurching around in the back as we weave through the narrow, choked streets, I can feel the pulse points in my neck and wrist jumping like crickets.

2:49 P.M. The wood-block floor in Emily's school hall was obviously installed with the express purpose of exposing late-arriving working mothers in heels. I tick-tock in at the moment when Angel Gabriel is breaking the big news to the Virgin Mary, who starts pulling the wool off the donkey sitting next to her. Mary is played by Genevieve Law, daughter of Alexandra Law, form representative and a Mother Superior—in other words, defiantly nonworking. There is serious competition among the Mothers Superior to secure leading roles in the production for their young. Trust me, they didn't give up that seat on the board or major TV series for little Joshua to play the innkeeper's brother in a Gap polo neck.

"A sheep was *perfect* for him last year," they cry, "but this Christmas we really feel he could tackle something a little more challenging!"

As the Three Wise Men—a wispy red-haired boy propelled by two little girls—walk across the stage with their presents for the Baby Jesus, the hall door opens behind us with a treacherous squeal. A hundred pairs of eyes swivel round to see a red-faced woman with a Tesco's carrier bag and a briefcase. Looks like Amy Redman's mum. As she edges, cringing and apologetic, into the back row of seats, Alexandra Law shushes her noisily. My instinctive sympathy for this fellow creature is outweighed almost immediately by an ugly swelling of gratitude that, thanks to her, I am no longer the last to arrive. (I don't want other working mothers to suffer unduly, truly I don't. I just need to know we're all screwing up about the same amount.)

Up on stage, a wobbly wail of recorders heralds the final carol. My angel is third from the left in the back row. On this big occasion, Emily has the same inky-eyed concentration, the same quizzical pucker of the brow she had coming out of the womb. I remember she looked round the delivery room for a couple of minutes, as if to say, No, don't tell me, I'll get it in a minute. This afternoon, flanked by fidgety boys, one of whom plainly needs the loo, my girl sings the carol without faltering over any of the words, and I feel a knock of pride in my rib cage.

Why are infants performing "Away in a Manger" in a headlong rush so much more affecting than the entire in-tune King's College Choir? I dig down into a bosky corner of my coat pocket and find a hankie.

3:41 P.M.   At the festive refreshments, there are a handful of fathers hiding behind video cameras, but the hall is aswarm with mothers, moths fluttering round the little lights of their lives. At school functions, other women always look like real mothers to me; I never feel I'm old enough for that title, or sufficiently well qualified. I can feel my body adopting exaggerated maternal gestures like a mime artist. The evidence that I am a mother, though, is holding tightly on to my left hand and insisting that I wear her halo in my hair. Emily is clearly relieved and grateful that Mummy made it; last year I had to drop out at the last minute when deal negotiations hit a critical phase and I had to jump on a plane to the States. I brought her a musical snow shaker of New York, snatched up in Saks Fifth Avenue, as a consolation present, but it was no consolation. The times you don't make it are the ones children remember, not the times you do.

Am anxious to slip away and call the office, but there is no avoiding Alexandra Law, who is accepting rave notices for Genevieve's Virgin Mary and for her own Bavarian *Liebkuchen*. Alexandra picks up one of my mince pies, jabs a dubious fingernail into the hill of icing sugar on top before pushing the whole lot into her mouth and announcing her verdict through a shower of crumbs. "Sen-say-sh'nul mince pies, Kate. Did you soak the fruit in brandy or grappa?"

"Oh, a dash of this and that, Alex, you know how it is."

She nods. "I was thinking of asking everyone to make stollen for next year. What d'you think? Do you have a good recipe?"

"No, but I know a supermarket that does."

"Ha-ha-ha-ha! Very good. Ha! Ha! Ha!"

Alexandra is the only woman I know who laughs as though it was written down. Mirthless, heaving Ted Heath shoulders. Any second now she will ask me if I've gone part-time yet.

"So, are you working part-time now? No? Still full-time. *Good heavens!* I don't know how you do it, honestly. I say, Claire, I was just saying to Kate, I don't know how she does it. Do you?"

———

7:27 P.M.   The strain of being an angel has taken its toll on Emily. She is so exhausted that I calculate I can turn over three pages of the bedtime story without her noticing. Must get on with that e-mail backlog. But just as I am skipping the pages, a suspicious eye snaps open.

"Mummy, you made a mistake."

"Did I?"

"You left out the bit where Piglet jumps in Kanga's pocket!"

"Oh, dear, did I?"

"Never mind, Mummy. We can just start at the beginning again."

8:11 P.M.   The answerphone that sits on the table next to the TV is full. Play messages. A West Country burr informs me that KwikToy is returning my call about undelivered Christmas presents. "Unfortunately, owing to unprecedented demand, the items will not now be with you until the New Year."

Christ. What's wrong with these people?

A message from my mother comes next and takes up most of the tape. Nervous of the technology, Mum still leaves pauses for the person at the other end to reply. She rang to say not to worry, she will manage fine without us over Christmas; somehow her reassurance is more piercing than any complaint could be. It's the knockout one-two that mothers have perfected down the centuries: first they make you feel guilty, and then you feel resentful at being made to feel guilty, which makes you feel even worse.

"I've put some books for Emily and Ben in the post and a little something for you and Richard. I hope they'll be the right sort of thing." She is afraid of not pleasing, in this as in so much else.

After my mother's wan reproachfulness, it's a relief to hear the voice of Jill Cooper-Clark wishing me a happy Christmas. Sorry she hasn't got organized with cards this year, been a bit dicky—laughter—although at least her new doctor looks like Dirk Bogarde. Sends her love and asks me to give her a call sometime.

Finally, I hear a voice so drained of warmth I barely recognize it: Janine, a former broker friend. Janine gave up work last year when her husband's firm floated on the stock market and Graham came into the kind of wealth that buys you a yacht called *Tabitha*, once owned by a cousin of Aristotle Onassis. When Janine was still working, we used to enjoy the battle-weary camaraderie of running a home while trying to make it across Man's Land avoiding sniper fire. These days, Janine does afternoon classes at the Chelsea Physic Garden on how to get the most out of your seasonal window box. She has winter and summer covers for her sofas, which get changed at the correct time of year, and lately she has arranged all the family photographs in padded albums, which sit on the coffee table in her drawing room exuding the mellow smells of leather and contentment. Last time I asked Janine what she was up to, she gave a little trill and said, "Oh, you know, just pottering." No, I don't know. Pottering and me, I don't think we've been introduced.

Janine is ringing to check if we're coming to their New Year's Eve dinner. She's sorry to bother us. She doesn't sound sorry. She sounds spitty with the indignation of a hostess scorned.

What New Year's dinner? A few minutes of excavating the hall table—tandoori leaflets, dead leaves, a single brown mitten—turns up an unopened pile of Christmas post. I riffle through the envelopes till I get to the one addressed in Janine's careful copperplate. Inside is a card photomontage of Graham, Janine, and their perfectly untroubled children plus an invitation to dinner. RSVP by December tenth.

I now do what I always do on such occasions: I blame Richard. (It doesn't have to be his fault, but someone has to be landed with the blame, or how is life to be tolerated?) Kneeling on the kitchen floor, Rich is making Ben a reindeer out of cardboard and what looks like the missing brown mitten. I tell him we are no longer even capable of turning down the events we will be unable to attend: our social ostracism is nearly complete. Am suddenly overcome with longing to be one of those women who reply promptly to invitations on thick creamy notepaper with a William Morris border. And in fountain pen, not some drought-stricken jade felt tip I have raided from Emily's pencil case.

Rich shrugs. "Come off it, Kate. You'd go mad."

Perhaps, but it would be nice to have the choice.

11:57 P.M.   The bath. My favorite place on earth. Leaning over the empty tub, I clear out the Pingu toys and the wrecked galleon, unstick the alphabet letters which, ever since the vowels got flushed down the loo, have formed angry Croat injunctions around the rim (*scrtzchk!*). I peel off the crusty half-dry Barbie flannel that has started to smell of something I vaguely remember as tadpole; and then, starting at one corner, I lift up the nonslip mat, whose suction cups cling for a second before yielding with an indignant burp.

Next, I ransack the cabinet, looking for a relaxing bath oil—lavender, sea cucumber, bergamot—but I am always out of destressors and have to settle for something with bubbles called Vitality in nuclear lime. Then I run the water hotter than you can bear, so hot that when I climb in my body momentarily mistakes it for cold. Lie back, nostrils flaring over the surface like an alligator. I look at the woman rapidly vanishing in the steamy mirror by my side and I think this is her time, her time alone, save for the odd overlooked Barney the dinosaur bobbing up suddenly between her knees with its serial-killer grin.

The bath is ancient, its porcelain riddled with gray-blue veins. We ran out of money after doing the kitchen so the house is in ascending order of crud: the higher up you go the lower the standards. Kitchen by Terence Conran, sitting room by Ikea, bathroom by Fungus the Bogeyman. But with my contact lenses out and in candlelight, the bathroom's leprous peeling speaks to me of some vestal Roman temple rather than five grand's worth of absent damp course.

As the bubbles evaporate on my hands, scaly pink islets are revealed along the knuckles. It's already got behind my right ear. Stress eczema, the nurse at work called it. "Can you think of any way to relieve some of the pressures in your life, Kate?" Oh, let's see now: a brain transplant, a lottery win, my husband reprogrammed to figure out that things left at the bottom of the stairs usually need to be carried to the top of the stairs.

Can't see how I can go on like this. Can't see how to stop, either. Can't help wondering if I was too hard on that Sri Lankan girl at the induction today, Momo Somebody. Seemed sweet enough. She asked me to be honest. Should I have been? Told her that the only way to get on at EMF is to act like one of the boys, and when you act like one of the boys they call you abrasive and difficult, so you act like a woman, and then they say you're emotional and difficult. *Difficult* being their word for everything that's not them. Well, she'll learn.

If I'd known at her age what I know now, would I ever have had children? Close my eyes and try to imagine a world without Emily and Ben: like a world without music or lightning.

Sink back under the water to let my thoughts float free, but they feel stuck to my brain like barnacles.

MUST REMEMBER

Talk with Paula outlining firm new approach to children's hair-cuts, timekeeping, etc. Talk with Rod Task outlining firm new approach to role with clients, i.e., *I am not their emergency geisha!* Pay rise: repeat after me, *I will not accept extra work without extra money!* Get quote for new stair carpet. Buy Christmas tree and stylish lights (John Lewis or Ikea?). Present for Richard (*How to Be a Domestic Goddess*?), In-laws (cheese barrel or alpine plants advertised in S. *Times* color supplement: where did I put the cutting?). Stocking fillers for E&B. Fruit jellies Uncle Alf. Travel sick sweets? Ask Paula collect dry cleaning. Personal shopper how much? Pelvic floor *squeeeeze*. Make icing for Christmas cake: too late, buy roll-on stuff. Cards stamps *First* class × 30. Wean Ben off dummy! Remember Roo!! Ring KwikToy useless bloody present co and threaten legal action. Nappies, bottles, *Toy Story* video, Smear test!!! Highlights. Hamster?

3

Happy Holidays

I CAN GET MYSELF and two children washed and dressed and out of the house in half an hour, I can juggle nine different currencies in five different time zones, I can make myself come with quiet efficiency, I can prepare and eat a stand-up supper while on the phone to the West Coast, I can read *Guess How Much I Love You?* to Ben scanning the prices on Teletext, but can I get a minicab to take me to the airport?

As part of an ongoing program of cutbacks, Edwin Morgan Forster will no longer send a car to deliver me to Heathrow. I must order my own. Last night I booked a local minicab, which this morning failed to show. When I rang to protest, the guy at the other end said he was very sorry but the soonest they could get a car to me was half an hour.

"It's a busy time of day, love."

I *know* it's a busy time of day. That's why I prebooked last night.

Says he thinks he may be able to get me something in twenty minutes. Hotly reject this insulting offer and slam phone down. Immediately regret it as all the other companies I call either don't have a car available or suggest an even more disastrous waiting time.

Am in despair when I spot a dirty bronze card sticking out from under the doormat. It's for a taxi company I've never heard of: Pegasus—Your Winged Driver. When I dial the number, the guy at the other end says he's coming right over. Relief is short-lived. This being Hackney, what turns up at the door is Pegasus—Your Stoned Driver. Parked at almost 45 degrees to the curb, Pegasus's chariot is a Nissan Sunny of impenetrable gloom hung about with veils of nicotine and hash. Climb in, but it's technically impossible to breathe in cab, so try to roll down window and stick head outside like a dog.

"Window he's not working," volunteers the driver, factually and without regret.

"And the seat belt?"

"Not working."

"You do realize that's illegal."

In the rearview mirror, Pegasus shoots me a pitying look that instructs me to get a life.

The cab not turning up made me so tense I had this stupid, stupid row with Richard. He found Paula's Xmas bonus check, which I'd hidden in Emily's lunch box. Said he simply couldn't understand why I spent more on the nanny's Christmas present than on the rest of the family put together.

I tried to explain. "Because if I don't keep Paula happy she will leave."

"Would that really be so bad, Katie?"

"Frankly, it would be easier if you left."

"Ah. I see."

Shouldn't have put it like that. Damned tiredness. Always makes you say what you don't mean to say, even if you feel it at the time. After that, Rich sat at the kitchen table pretending to have found something fascinating to read in *Architectural Digest* while managing to look like Trevor Howard at the end of *Brief Encounter*—all chin-up decency and glittery eyes.

Wouldn't even look at me when I said goodbye. Then Ben stood up in his high chair and started yodeling for a hug. No. Sorry. Not in a clean suit: the state of him! Smeared with jam and apricot *fromage frais*, like his own personal sunrise.

The cab stops and starts and stops again along the Euston Road. If this is one of London's main arteries, then London needs a coronary bypass. Its citizens sit in their cars, hearts furring up with fury.

Once we're past King's Cross, I open my post. There's a card from Mum enclosing a magazine's Yuletide supplement, "26 Recipes for a Magical Stress-Free Christmas!" Flick through pages in mounting disbelief. How can anything stress-free involve caramelizing a shallot?

We continue to crawl westward, over the flyover and past the brick-pink semis, like mile upon mile of gaping dentures. When I used to live in a house like that, Christmas was still a pretty simple affair. It was a tree, a pimply turkey, satsumas trapped in an orange net, maybe some dates clinging gummily together in a palm-tree canoe and a bumper tin of Quality Street eaten by the whole family in front of Morecambe and Wise. Your big present was always waiting for you downstairs next to the tree—a doll's house, roller skates, maybe a bike with training wheels or a bell—and there was a stocking whose thrilling misshapen weight your feet discovered at the end of the bed. But Christmas, like everything else, has moved up a gear. Now it's productions of *The Nutcracker* (book tickets in August) and Kelly Bronze. When I first heard the name, I assumed Kelly was one of those inflatable *Baywatch* babes, but she turns out to be the only kind of turkey that's worth eating anymore. And once you've spent an hour on the phone being held in a queue in order to beg the supermarket to put you on the waiting list for Kelly, you have to get the bird home and stuff her. According to my Yuletide supplement, stuffing, which was once stale bread crumbs with diced onion and a spoonful of fusty sage, has evolved into "porcini butter with red rice and cranberry to revive jaded palates."

I don't believe we had palates in the seventies; we had sweet teeth and heartburn that you eased by sucking lozenges the color and texture of gravestones. It's a good joke when you think about it, isn't it? Just as women were fleeing the role of homemaker in their millions, there was suddenly food that was worth cooking. Think of all the great stuff you could be making, Kate, if you were ever in your kitchen to make it.

8:43 A.M. Pegasus has chosen a "quick" back route to Heathrow. So, with one hour twenty-two minutes to takeoff, we are sitting outside a row of halal butchers in Southall. Feel my heart revving, foot jammed on an invisible accelerator.

"Look, can't you go any faster? I absolutely *have* to make up time."

A young guy in white cotton pajamas steps out into the road in front of us, a lamb the size of a child slung over his shoulder. My driver brakes suddenly and from the front of the car comes a laconic drawl. "Last time I looked, lady, running people over is still against the law."

Close eyes and concentrate on calming down. Things will feel much more under control if I make efficient use of the time: call

KwikToy ("Round the Clock Fun!") on mobile to complain about no-show of vital Christmas presents.

"Thank you for choosing KwikToy. We are sorry, you are held in a queue. Your call will be answered shortly." Typical.

Start to work my way through torn-out Yellow Pages list of north London pet shops. It comes as no surprise to learn there is a national shortage of baby hamsters, though there might be one left in Walthamstow. Am I interested? Yes.

When I finally get through to KwikToy, clueless operative seems reluctant to admit they have any record of my order. Tell him I am a major shareholder in his company and we are about to review our investment.

"Awright," he concedes, "there have been some delivery difficulties owing to unprecedented demand."

I point out that the demand can hardly be described as unprecedented.

"The birth of the little baby Jesus. Been celebrating that one for two thousand years. Toys and Christmas, Christmas and toys. Ring any bells?"

"Would you be asking for a voucher, miss?"

"No, I would not be asking for a voucher. I am asking for my toys to be delivered *immediately* so my children will have something to open on Christmas Day."

There is a pause, a beep and an echoey shout: "Oy, Jeff, some posh tart's doing her nut on the phone about the Goldilocks porridge set and the push-along sheepdog. Whatmygonnatella?"

9:17 A.M. Arrive at Heathrow with time to spare. Decide to try to make it up to the driver for yelling. Ask his name.

"Winston," he offers suspiciously.

"Thanks, Winston. That was a really good route. I'm Kate, by the way. Such a great name, Winston. As in Churchill?"

He savors the moment before replying: "As in Silcott."

9:26 A.M. Barging through a choked Departure Lounge, remember something else I have forgotten. Need to call home. Mobile not in service. Why not? Try pay phone, which eats three pound coins and fails to connect me while repeating the message: "Thank you for choosing British Telecom."

Finally get through on credit-card phone next to the boarding
desk, watched by three members of staff in navy uniforms.

"Richard, hello? Whatever you do, don't forget the stockings."

"Lingerie?"

"What?"

"Stockings. Is there a lingerie angle here, Katie? Suspenders, black
lace, three inches of creamy thigh, or are we talking boring old Santa
gift receptacle?"

"Richard, have you been drinking?"

"It's an idea, certainly." As he puts the phone down, I swear I can
hear Paula offering Emily a Hubba Bubba.

My daughter is not allowed bubble gum.

To: Candy Stratton
From: Kate Reddy in Stockholm

Client threatening to drop us on account of worrying dip in fund
performance. Spun them a line about Edwin Morgan Forster asset
managers being like Bjorn Borg: brilliant baseline stayers playing
percentage shots and aiming for consistent victories over the long
term, not flashy burnout artists going for quick profits and then
double-faulting. Seemed to buy it. God knows why.

Kept popping out of Bengt Bergman boardroom to executive
washroom, locking self in cubicle and using mobile to call pet shops in
Walthamstow. Up until three days ago, Emily's letters to Santa made
no mention of hamster, now suddenly upgraded to Number One item.

Swedish clients all have names like a bad hand of Scrabble. Sven
Sjostrom kept spearing rollmops off my plate at lunch and saying he
was a passionate believer in "closer European union."

Trust me to get only non-PC man in Scandinavia. Yeurk, K8 xxxxx

---

To: Kate Reddy
From: Candy Stratton

Sven Will I See U Again?

Sven Will We Share Precious Moments?

go for it, hon, it will relax you! luv Cystitis xxx

To: Candy Stratton
From: Kate Reddy

That is NOT FUNNY. Remember, I am a happily married woman. Well,
I'm married anyway.

To: Kate Reddy
From: Debra Richardson

Have just had unspeakable humiliation at hands—or rather mouth—of
hateful school secretary at Piper Place (i know, i know, should stop this
education madness). Yes, Ruby could be assessed for a place for
2002, "But I must warn you, Mrs. Richardson, that there are over a
hundred little girls on our list and we have a strong siblings policy."

Do you have any Semtex? These smug cows have got to be stopped.

What's new??

To: Debra Richardson
From: Kate Reddy

Have not put Em down for school yet. By the time I get round to it, will
probably have to have sex with the headmaster to have any chance of
getting her in. . . . More pressing problem: 2 days to wean Ben off
dummy 'cause mother-in-law thinks this sucking device is tool of the
devil, only used by gypsies or chain-smoking lowlifes who "park
children in front of the video." What else to do with children in
Yorkshire?

Have found hamster for Emily. Apparently female hamsters v. bad-
tempered and sometimes bite or eat their young. Now why would
that be?

2:17 A.M. Blizzard. Flight home delayed. Precious seconds set aside for last-minute shopping in London being eaten up. Scour Stockholm airport shop for Christmas presents. Which would Rich prefer, wind-dried reindeer or seasonal video entitled *Swedish Teen Honeys in the Snow*? Still refusing to buy Emily vulgar messy Baby Wee-Wee as seen on breakfast TV. Compromise on the local Swedish Barbie-type doll—wholesome individual, probably a Social Democrat, wearing peacekeeper khaki.

———————

CHRISTMAS EVE. OFFICES OF EDWIN MORGAN FORSTER. I should have known where my pay negotiations were going when Rod Task came round the back of my chair, air-patted my shoulder three times like a vet preparing a cat for a jab and described me as "a highly valued member of the team." It was midafternoon, the dregs of the day, and the sky over Broadgate was the color of tea.

Rod explained that there would be no bonus this year—the bonus I have been counting on to finish the building work on the house and for so much else. Times were tough for everybody, he said, but the really great news was they were giving me a major new challenge.

"We think you're the person to do client servicing, Katie, 'cause you do it so damn well. Anyways, you got the best legs."

A burly and curly Aussie, with a voice other guys use to get the attention of a bartender, when Rod first heaved his bulk over from Sydney to join EMF as Director of Marketing three and a half years ago—brought in to put some lead in the English firm's propelling pencil—I really thought I'd have to leave. His inability to look me in the eye—and not just because I'm two inches taller—the way he would comment on parts of my body as though they were on special offer, his habit of ending every meeting with an injunction to "Get out there and kick the fucking tires!" After a few weeks, when Candy sweetly asked Rod for an English translation of this phrase, he looked perplexed for a few seconds, then gave a broad grin. "Screw the client for every penny you can!"

So I was going to have to leave. But then Emily hit the Terrible Twos and I bought a book called *Toddler Taming*. It was a revelation. The advice on how to deal with small angry immature people who have no idea of limits and were constantly testing their mother applied perfectly to my boss. Instead of treating him as a superior, I began handling him as though he were a tricky small boy. Whenever he was about to do something naughty, I would do my best to distract him; if I wanted him to do something, I always made it look like it was his idea.

Anyway, Rod says that from today I assume responsibility for the Salinger Foundation. Based in New York, chief executive by the name of Jack Abelhammer, two-hundred-million-dollar business, needs someone of my caliber. I'll be able to familiarize myself with the portfolio over the holidays, of course, plus I will continue to baby-sit all my old clients while Rod finds the right person to take over from me.

I ask Rod what Abelhammer is like.

"Good swing."

"I beg your pardon?"

"Short game needs work."

"Oh. Golf."

"Whatcha think I'm talking about, Katie, sex?"

The holiday doesn't strictly begin till close of play today, but the office is practically deserted; unofficially, we are now in the limbo between boozy lunch and alcoholic tea. When I get back to my desk, Candy is perched on the heater under the window with her legs stretched out and resting on top of my chair. She is wearing an amazing cantilevered scarlet blouse and purple fishnets and there is gold tinsel in her hair.

"OK, let me guess," she says. "He took a crap on you and you offered to wipe his ass."

"Excuse me." I grab her ankles and spin her feet off the chair. "Actually, things went very well. Rod thinks my client-handling skills are a major asset, so as a vote of confidence they are giving me this big foundation all to myself."

"Right." When Candy laughs you get a glimpse of a mouthful of enviable American teeth.

"Don't look at me like that."

"Kate, a major vote of confidence round here always comes with at least four zeros on the end of it, you know that. What else'd he say?"

I don't have time to reply because Candy puts a finger to her lips as Chris Bunce, bastard in residence, sways past us on his way to the Gents with a long lunch under his belt. A major cokehead, Bunce manages to look both skinny and bloated. Since I made it clear to

him, quite politely, that I wasn't interested in the contents of his box-
ers, the sexual tension between us has given way to teasing skirmishes
with occasional rounds of live ammunition being fired when I get a
deal he wants. (Guys like Bunce see rejection as an insult that must be
repaid with compound interest—like the Third World debt.)

Candy tips her head towards his retreating figure. "Lot of dirt getting into EMF one way and another. D'you offer to clean the office
for them too?"

"What do you take me for? Rod said no one was getting a bonus."

"And you believed him?" Candy closes her eyes and sighs a smile.
"That's what I love about you, Kate. Smartest female economist since
Maynard Keynes, and you still think when they mug you they're
doing you a favor."

"Candy, Maynard Keynes was a man."

She shakes her head and the tinsel sends out prickles of light. "He
was not. He was a fruit. Way I see it, we women have to claim all the
guys in history with a strong feminine side as ours."

6:09 P.M. Packing the car for the journey up north to my parents-
in-law takes at least two hours. There is the first hour during which
Richard pieces together a pleasing jigsaw of baby belongings in the
boot. (Louis XIV traveled lighter than Ben.) Then comes the moment where he has to find the key that unlocks the luggage box that
sits like an upturned boat on our roof. "Where did we put it, Kate?"
After ten minutes of swearing and emptying every drawer in the
house, Richard finds the key in the pocket of his jacket.

After Rich has told me to get the kids in the car "right now," there
follows twenty minutes of frantic unloading as he "just makes sure" he
has packed the sterilizer, which he "knows for a fact" he wedged next
to the spare tire. This is followed by a furious repacking, punctuated
by *fuck-its,* when items are squidged on top of one another any old
how and the remnants are jammed into all available foot space front
and back. The Easi-wipe changing mat, the Easi-clip portable high
chair with its companion piece, the vermilion Easi-assemble porta-
cot. Bibs, melamine Thomas the Tank Engine bowls, sleep suits.
Emily's blankie—a tragic hank of yellow wool that looks as though it
has been run over several times by a heavy goods vehicle. An entire

bestiary of nocturnal comforters: Ben's beloved Roo, a sheep, a hippopotamus in a tutu, a wombat that is an eerie Roy Hattersley double. Ben's dummies (to be hidden from Richard's parents at all costs). Emily's surprise hamster is stashed in the boot.

Strapped into their seats in the back of the car like cosmonauts awaiting blastoff, Emily and Ben's contented bickering soon gives way to hand-to-hand combat. In a moment of weakness—when do I have a moment of strength?—I have opened the chocolate Santa dispenser meant for Christmas morning and given them a couple of foil-wrapped pieces each to keep them quiet. As a result, Emily, who fifteen minutes ago was wearing white pajamas, now looks like a dalmatian, with a dark-brown muzzle around her mouth and cocoa smudges everywhere else.

Richard, who has a heroic indifference to the cleanliness and general presentation of his offspring for eleven and a half months of the year, suddenly asks me why Ben and Emily look such a mess. What's his mother going to think?

Swipe at children with moist travel tissues. Four hours on the A-1 motorway lie ahead of us. Car is so overloaded it sways like a ship.

"Are we still in England?" demands an incredulous voice from the back.

"Yes."

"Are we at Grandma's house yet?"

"No."

"But I *want* to be at Grandma's house."

By Hatfield, both children are performing a fugue for scream and whimper. Crank up the *Carols from Kings* tape and Rich and I sing along gustily. (Rich is the descant specialist while I take the Jessye Norman part.) Near Peterborough, eighty miles out of London, a small nagging thought manages to wriggle its way clear from the compost heap that presently comprises the contents of my head.

"Rich, you did remember to pack Roo?"

"I didn't know I was meant to be remembering Roo. I thought you were remembering Roo."

Like any other family, the Shattocks have their Christmas traditions. One tradition is that I buy all the presents for my side of the family and I buy all the presents for our children and our two godchildren and I buy Richard's presents and presents for Richard's parents and his brother Peter and Peter's wife Cheryl and their three kids and Richard's Uncle Alf, who drives across from Matlock every Boxing Day and is keen on rugby league and can only manage soft centers. If Richard remembers, and depending on late opening hours, he buys a present for me.

"What have we got for Dad, then?" Rich will inquire on the drive up to Yorkshire. The marital *we* which means you which means me.

I buy the wrapping paper and the Sellotape and I wrap all the presents. I buy the cards and a large sheet of second-class stamps. By the time I have written all the cards and forged Rich's signature and written something warm yet lighthearted about time flying and how we'll definitely be in touch in the New Year (a lie), it is too late for second-class mail, so I join the queue at the post office to buy first-class stamps. Then I fight my way through Selfridge's food hall to buy cheese and those little Florentines that Barbara likes.

And then, when we get to Barbara and Donald's house, we unpack the stuff from the car and we put all the presents under the tree and the food and the drink in the kitchen, and they chorus, "Oh, Richard, thank you for getting the wine. You shouldn't have gone to all that trouble."

Is it possible to die of ingratitude?

MIDNIGHT MASS, ST. MARY'S, WROTHLY.   The grass on the village green is so full of ice tonight it's almost musical: we clink and chink our way from the Shattocks' old mill house to the tiny Norman church. Inside, the pews are full, the air dense and dank and flavored with winey breath. I know you're meant to disapprove of the drunks who only come to church this one time in the year, but standing here next to Rich, I think how much I like them, envy them even. Their noisy attempts at hush, the sense they've come in search of heat and light and a little human kindness.

I hold it together, I really do, until we get to that line in "O Little Town of Bethlehem" when I have to press both gloves to my eyes:

"Above thy deep and dreamless sleep the silent stars go by."

4

Christmas Day

SATURDAY, 5:37 A.M. WROTHLY, YORKSHIRE. It's still dark outside. The four of us are in bed together in a sprawling tentacular cuddle. Emily, half mad with Santa lust, is tearing off wrapping paper. Ben is playing peepo with the debris. I give Richard a packet of wind-dried reindeer, two pairs of Swedish socks (oatmeal), a five-day wine-tasting course in Burgundy, and *How to Be a Domestic Goddess* (joke). Barbara and Donald give me a wipable Liberty print apron and *How to Be a Domestic Goddess* (not joke).

Richard gives me: (1) Agent Provocateur underwear—red bra with raised black satin spots and demitasse cup over which nipples jut like helmeted medieval warriors peeking above parapet; also, a suspender/knicker device apparently trimmed with trawlerman's netting, and (2) Membership of National Trust.

Both fall into category of what I think of as PC presents: Please Change. Emily gives me a fantastic travel clock. Instead of an alarm, it has a message recorded by her: "Wake up, Mummy; wake up, sleepyhead!"

We give Emily a hamster (female, but to be called Jesus), a Barbie bike, a Brambly Hedge doll's house, a remote-control robot dog and a lot of other stuff made out of plastic that she doesn't need. Emily is thrilled with the Peacekeeper Barbie I snatched up in Stockholm Duty Free until she opens Paula's present: Baby Wee-Wee, which I have expressly forbidden.

Risking hysteria, we try to get most of the kids' gifts unwrapped upstairs so that my parents-in-law will not be appalled by reckless metropolitan surfeit ("Throwing your money about") and the outrageous spoiling of the younger generation ("In my day, you counted yourself lucky to get a doll with a china head and an orange").

Some things are harder to keep quiet. It's difficult to pretend to grandparents, for instance, that your child is just an occasional video watcher when, during breakfast, she gives a word-perfect rendition of every song from *The Little Mermaid,* adding brightly that the DVD version has an extra tune. At the table, I sense another source of conflict when I remind Emily to stop playing with the salt.

"Emily, Grandpa asked you to put that down."

"No, I didn't," says Donald mildly. "I *told* her to put it down. That's the difference between my generation and yours, Kate: we told, you ask."

A few minutes later, standing by the Aga stirring scrambled eggs, I am suddenly aware of Barbara hovering by my side. She finds it hard to conceal her disbelief at the contents of the saucepan. "Goodness, do the children like their eggs dry?"

"Yes, this is the way I always do them."

"Oh."

Barbara is obsessed with the food intake of my family, whether it's the children's lack of vegetables or my own strange unwillingness to plow through three three-course meals a day. "You need to build your strength up, Katharine." And no Shattock family gathering would be complete without my mother-in-law pressing me into the African violet nook next to the pantry and hissing, "Richard looks thin, Katharine. Isn't Richard looking *thin*?"

When Barbara says *thin* it immediately becomes a fat word: hefty, breathless, accusing. I shut my eyes and try to summon reserves of patience and understanding I don't have. The woman standing before me equipped my husband with the DNA that gave him the lifelong figure of a Biro refill, and thirty-six years later she blames me. Is this fair? I rise above such slights on my wifeliness, what there is of it.

"But Richard *is* thin," I protest. "Rich was skinny when we met. That's one of the things I loved about him."

"He was always slim," concedes Barbara, "but now there's nothing left of him. Cheryl said as soon as she saw him get out of the car, 'Doesn't Richard look run down, Barbara?'"

Cheryl is my sister-in-law. Before she married Peter, Richard's accountant brother, Cheryl was something in the Halifax building society. Since she had the first of her three boys in 1989, Cheryl has become a member of what my friend Debra calls the Muffia—the powerful stay-at-home cabal of organized mums. Both Cheryl and Barbara treat men as though they were livestock who need careful husbandry. No Christmas in the Shattock family would be complete without Cheryl asking me if my Joseph cashmere roll-neck is from JCPenney, or if it's really all right that Rich should be upstairs bathing the children *by himself.*

Peter is a lot less help with the family than Richard, but over the years I have come to see that Cheryl enjoys and even encourages her husband's uselessness. Peter plays the valuable role in Cheryl's life of the Cross I Have to Bear. Every martyr needs a Peter who, given time, can be trained up to not recognize his own underpants.

Things I take for granted at home in London are viewed up here as egalitarianism gone mad. "Somme," says Richard in grim triumph, walking through the kitchen holding aloft a bulging nappy sack whose apricot scent is fighting a losing battle to subdue the stink within. (Rich has evolved a classification system for Ben's nappies—a minor incident is a Tant Pis, an average load is a Croque Manure, while an all-out seven-wipes job is a Somme. Once, but only once, there was a Krakatoa. Fair enough, but not in a Greek airport.)

"Of course, in our day the fathers didn't pitch in at all," says Barbara, flinching. "You wouldn't get Donald going near a nappy. Drive a mile to avoid one."

"Richard's fantastic," I say carefully. "I couldn't manage without him."

Barbara takes a red onion and quarters it fiercely. "You've got to look after them a bit, men. Delicate flowers," she muses, pressing the blade down till the onion cries softly to itself. "Can you give that gravy a stir for me, Katharine?" Cheryl comes in and starts defrosting cheese straws and vol-au-vent cases for tomorrow's drinks party.

I feel so alone when Barbara and Cheryl are twittering together in the kitchen, even though I'm standing right there. I reckon this must be how it was for centuries: women doing the doing and exchanging conspiratorial glances and indulgent sighs about the men. But I never joined the Muffia; I don't know the code, the passwords, the special handshakes. I expect a man—my man—to do women's work, because if he doesn't I can't do a man's work. And up here in Yorkshire, the pride I feel in managing, the fact that I can and do make our lives stay